QUIZ BOOK 2014

Derek O'Brien was born in Kolkata. He began his professional career as a journalist for *Sportsworld* magazine but soon shifted to advertising. After working for a number of very successful years as Creative Head of Ogilvy, Derek decided to focus all his energy and talent in his passion—quizzing.

Today, Derek O'Brien is Asia's best-known quizmaster and CEO of Derek O'Brien & Associates. He is the host of the longest-running game show on Indian television, the Bournvita Quiz Contest, for which he was voted the Best Anchor of a Game Show at the Indian Television Academy Awards for three years in a row. Always innovating and keeping abreast of the times, he is also credited with having conducted the first quiz on Twitter in 2010.

In 2011, he was voted to the Rajya Sabha as a Member of Parliament and is the Chief Whip of the Trinamool Congress in the Rajya Sabha. In 2012, he addressed the United Nations General Assembly.

He has written several best-selling reference and quiz books.

Stay in touch with Derek through his website www.derek.in, or on Twitter where his handle is @quizderek.

QUIZ BOOK 2014

DEREK O'BRIEN

RUPA

Published by
Rupa Publications India Pvt. Ltd 2014
7/16, Ansari Road, Daryaganj
New Delhi 110002

Sales Centres:

Allahabad Bengaluru Chennai
Hyderabad Jaipur Kathmandu
Kolkata Mumbai

ISBN: 978-81-291-3516-2

First impression 2014

10 9 8 7 6 5 4 3 2 1

To my supremely talented colleagues at
Derek O'Brien & Associates who make me
look way better than I am

CONTENTS

CELEBRATING BQC

Addressing the United Nations General Assembly is a rare honour. Delivering a speech in the hallowed portals of the Parliament is a unique privilege. The experiences of the last three years since I entered the Rajya Sabha as a Member of Parliament have been truly fulfilling and gratifying. Equally gratifying were the last twenty-two years interacting with students and asking questions on the sets of the iconic Bournvita Quiz Contest (BQC). It has been a most rewarding and humbling journey—one which I continue to enjoy and cherish.

The legendary programme in its radio avatar was hosted by the late Hamid Sayani. After his demise, his brother Ameen Sayani took over. Ameen saab is now in his eighties and lives a quiet life in Mumbai.

Cadbury (Mondelez India Foods Limited) and Derek O'Brien & Associates got together in 1992 to launch BQC in a new television avatar. Till then, it had been aired only on the radio and, though I had quite a number of stage shows under my belt, I was a newbie to television. So we didn't really know how TV viewers would embrace a quiz show.

Now, looking back twenty-two years later, there

is a deep sense of fulfillment. BQC was launched as an English programme, but has changed with the times. To reach a much larger audience, the multi-award winning Bournvita Quiz Contest is now a bilingual show in English and Hindi with the superbly talented Saumya Tandon as my co-quizmaster.

The growing popularity of BQC encouraged us to launch the show in Tamil in 2013. My co-quizmaster in this is the young and bubbly Nisha Krishnan, who is helping me take baby steps in Tamil.

As exciting as the television shows are the city finals that we conduct in eighty cities, hosted by my brilliant colleagues from Derek O'Brien & Associates.

But the real heroes and torch bearers of this legendary programme for the past two decades are not us, but the principals, teachers, parents and students for their continued support.

Thank you ever so much for making the Bournvita Quiz Contest what it is today. It is thanks to you that BQC has endured the test of TRPs and changing times. As they say in cricket: 'Form is temporary, class is permanent.'

This book is a compilation of the best questions asked on the latest season of BQC. It is a small tribute to each viewer who flicks the remote on Sunday mornings to watch the brightest minds engage in intellectual combat. We are humbled by your love and hope you will enjoy this brand new addition to the BQC quiz book series.

With every good wish,
Derek O'Brien

FOREWORD

As the Bournvita Quiz Contest enters its forty-third year, it gives me immense pleasure in introducing to you *BQC Quiz Book 2014*.

Since its launch in 1948, Cadbury (Mondelez India Foods Limited) Bournvita has been one of India's most loved and trusted brands. For over six decades, the brand has been an enduring symbol of mental and physical health and all-round development. In 1972, Cadbury (Mondelez India Foods Limited) introduced the Bournvita Quiz Contest as a radio programme. Following its tremendous success on radio, the programme found a new avatar on television in 1994. After a hiatus of a few years and following the compelling public movement to 'Bring BQC Back', 2011 saw the return of India's favourite quiz contest to national television.

This show has touched the lives of over 12 lakh children and millions of loyal viewers through its 600+ television episodes. A number of reputed personalities and celebrities from the fields of cinema, music, sports and politics have also made special appearances on the show.

BQC Quiz Book 2014 is a selection of the very best

questions asked on the latest season of this iconic show. So if you think you have an unquenchable thirst for knowledge, I am sure you will enjoy this book!

I would like to take this opportunity to thank the team from Derek O'Brien & Associates for producing this book. I would also like to thank the millions of viewers, students, principals and teachers for their love and support, which in turn has made the Bournvita Quiz Contest a household name!

Happy Quizzing!

Manu Anand
President, India and South Asia,
Mondelez International

HALL OF FAME

PAST WINNERS OF THE BOURNVITA
QUIZ CONTEST

1994-1995, Mumbai

Campion High School, Mumbai
Balakrishnan Sivaraman, Sudhanshu Bhuwalka

1995-1996, Mumbai

Kendriya Vidyalaya, Powai, Mumbai
Eipy Koshy, Gourav Shah

1996-1997, Mumbai

Bombay International High School, Mumbai
Nirica Borges, Advait Behara

1997, Mumbai

Mount Saint Mary's School, New Delhi
Joe Christy, Maninder Singh Jessel

1997-1998, Mumbai

Bombay Scottish High School, Mumbai
Shaambhavi Pandyaa, Rahul Lalmalani

1998, Mumbai

Sacred Heart Convent School, Jamshedpur
Ela Verma, Lavanya Raghavan

1998-1999, Mumbai

Indian School Al Ghubra, Muscat
Anand Raghavan, Hitesh Kanvatirtha

1999, Mumbai

Maneckji Cooper High School, Mumbai
Ipsita Bandopadhyay, Gourav Bhattacharya

1999-2000, Mumbai

Chettinad Vidyashram, Chennai
Siddharth, Karthik Das

2000-2001, Mumbai

Bharatiya Vidya Bhavan, Hyderabad
Ananya Bhaskar, Aksha Anand

2001 September, Mumbai

Brightlands, Dehradun
Ankur Bharadwaj, Shray Sharma

2001 December, Mumbai

Little Flower High School, Hyderabad
G. Mithilesh, K Siddharth Reddy

2002 February, Bentota, Sri Lanka

G.D. Birla Centre For Education, Kolkata
Namrata Basu, Rituparna Dey

2002 June, Mumbai

Kerala Samajam Public School, Jamshedpur
Saurav Biswas, Kunal Mohan

2002 September, Mumbai

Jamnabai Narsee School, Mumbai
Sharan Narayanan, Vishnu Shrest

2003 January, Kerala

Naval Public High School, Mumbai
Apoorva Sharma, Abhishek Pandit

2003 May, Kolkata

St. Patrick's Higher Secondary School, Asansol
Pushpen Dasgupta, Shamik Ray

2003 October, Sangla

St. Agnes Loreto Day School, Lucknow
Aastha Srivastava, Illa Gupta

2004 February, Swabhumi, Kolkata

Apeejay School, Jalandhar
Mohit Thukral, Sahil Sareen

2004 May, Goa

Springdales School, Delhi
Anirudh Sridhar, B. Anuraag

2004 July, Indian Military Academy, Dehradun

The Mother's International School, Delhi
Krittika Adhikary, Milind Ganjoo

2004 November, Kolkata

Amity International, New Delhi
Aishwarya Singhal, Adarsh Modi

2005 February, Kolkata

St. Kabir, Ahmedabad
Yogarshi Vyas, Helish Sharma

2005 May, Kolkata

Brightlands, Dehradun
Akshay Sharma, Avantika Singh

2005 August, Kolkata

Amity International, New Delhi
Utkarsh Johari, Aishwarya Singhal

2006 July, Kolkata

Riverdale High School, Dehradun
Kartikeya Panwar, Sumit Nair

2006 November, Kolkata

Seth Jaipuria School, Lucknow
Ratnaksha Lele, Ananya Kumar Singh

2011 August, Kolkata

Amity International School, Noida
Kripi Badonia, Shinjini Biswas

2012 January, Kolkata

Birla Vidya Niketan, New Delhi
Anusha Malhotra, Nitya Bansal

2013 January, Kolkata

Vidyaniketan Public School (Ullal), Bengaluru
Shashank Niranjan Gowda, Mainak Mandal

CREDITS

SENIOR RELATIONSHIP ASSOCIATES	Heena Ade (Israni)
	Sheldon Alliew
	Aubrey Whyte
	Dipankar Rao
	Calvin Tully
	Laressa Gomez
RELATIONSHIP ASSOCIATES	Durjoy Guha
	Conrad Pote
	Daniel Johns
	Fionna Sayers
	Tapan Roy
	Natasha Gasper
	Shaun Ward
	Ezekiel Mani
	Pritha Ghosh
	Doyson Gomes
	Nigel Salters
	AVNS Prasad
SENIOR DESIGN ASSOCIATE	Mahua Basu
SENIOR FINANCE ASSOCIATE	Kalyanmoy Hazra
SENIOR PRODUCTION ASSOCIATES	Sreevalsa Menon
	Shane Baptiste
PRODUCTION ASSOCIATES	Vinu Joseph
	Supriyo Nandi
	Victor Bhat
HINDI SCRIPT	Rahul
HINDI TRANSLATOR	Rajneesh Kaushal
CREATIVE (POST)	Vivek Iyer

EDITORS	Bhavin M. Patel
	Pradeep Jha
	Ratan Jha
MUSIC	Shankar, Ehsaan, Loy
SET DESIGN & FABRICATION	Kosmos India
SHOT AT	Purple Movie Town
PRODUCTION ASSISTANTS	Ananta Behera
	Pabitra Ghosh
	Mrinal Chakraborty
	Indrajit Saha
	Bipin Kumar Jha
	Sudip Dey

HISTORY

1. What did the Raja of Sikkim gift the British on 1 February 1835?
   a) Mount Everest
   b) Kaziranga National Park
   c) Darjeeling
   d) Taj Mahal

2. What measured 1,500 km in length from Sonar Gaon in Bengal to the Sindhu River in the west?
   a) Ganges
   b) Deccan Plateau
   c) Grand Trunk Road
   d) Great Wall of China

3. What animal adorned most of Tipu Sultan's possessions?
   a) King cobra
   b) Butterfly
   c) Tiger
   d) Camel

4. Who spent his last one hundred and forty-four days at Old Birla House on No. 5, Tees January Marg, New Delhi?
    a) Mahatma Gandhi
    b) Jawaharlal Nehru
    c) Swami Vivekananda
    d) Vallabhbhai Patel

5. In which state is Chetak Samadhi, a memorial to Maharana Pratap's horse?
    a) Gujarat
    b) Rajasthan
    c) Maharashtra
    d) Madhya Pradesh

6. In 326 BC, who did Ambhi give troops in return for aid against Porus?
    a) Alexander the Great
    b) Napoleon
    c) Mahmud of Ghazni
    d) Tamerlane

7. What title was given to the prime minister in Shivaji's Council of Ministers?
    a) Peshwa
    b) Alamgir
    c) Chhatrapati
    d) Maharana

8. In 1933, which word was first used in a pamphlet *Now or Never*?

a) Pakistan
b) Bharat
c) Inquilab
d) Swaraj

9. In 1941, whose arrival in Berlin to seek Hitler's help did Goebbels' radio service announce?
   a) Jawaharlal Nehru
   b) Subhas Chandra Bose
   c) Mahatma Gandhi
   d) Rabindranath Tagore

10. Who hoisted the Indian flag at Red Fort on 15 August, 1947?
    a) Jawaharlal Nehru
    b) Indira Gandhi
    c) Vallabhbhai Patel
    d) Subash Chandra Bose

11. Which princely state's currency was designated as the Osmania Sicca?
    a) Hyderabad
    b) Patiala
    c) Gwalior
    d) Bhopal

12. Which was the eighth month of the early Roman republican calendar?
    a) September
    b) October
    c) November
    d) December

13. Who gave the name Akbarabad to Agra in honour of his grandfather?
    a) Shah Jahan
    b) Aurangzeb
    c) Humayun
    d) Babur

14. Whose tomb lies at a distance of two kilometres west of Haldighati?
    a) Chetak
    b) Bucephalus
    c) Humayun
    d) Shivaji

15. After her first son was born in 304 BC, Queen Subhadrangi said that her life was then without sorrow. What was her son's name?
    a) Shivaji
    b) Humayun
    c) Chandragupta
    d) Ashoka

16. Whose voyages of discovery have been immortalised in Portugal's patriotic poem *The Lusiads*?
    a) Ibn Battuta
    b) Ferdinand Magellan
    c) Vasco da Gama
    d) Marco Polo

17. At which monument's base is the memorial Amar Jawan Jyoti?

a) Gateway of India
b) India Gate
c) Shahid Minar
d) Red Fort

18. Which famous person was born at Shivneri hillfort near Junnar town, about eighty-five km north of Pune in 1627 or 1630?
a) Tipu Sultan
b) Shivaji
c) Aurangzeb
d) Babur

19. In 1869, Auguste Bartholdi designed a statue of a woman with a torch, named 'Egypt Brings Light to Asia' as a lighthouse for the Suez Canal. When this project failed, which famous structure did he complete in 1886?
a) Eiffel Tower
b) Statue of Liberty
c) Leaning Tower of Pisa
d) Pieta

20. In 1893, which country's police force issued the world's first car number plates?
a) USA
b) Germany
c) France
d) Russia

21. Who wrote the book *Painting as a Pastime*?
    a) Adolf Hitler
    b) Albert Einstein
    c) Winston Churchill
    d) Mahatma Gandhi

22. What was built by Sawai Jai Singh II in Delhi, Jaipur, Ujjain, Varanasi and Mathura?
    a) Hawa Mahal
    b) Jantar Mantar
    c) Amer Fort
    d) Neemrana Fort

23. Which Mughal emperor built the Buland Darwaza to mark his victory over Gujarat?
    a) Akbar
    b) Humayun
    c) Jahangir
    d) Shah Jahan

24. Who was the last Tirthankara of Jainism?
    a) Sathya Sai Baba
    b) Buddha
    c) Guru Nanak
    d) Mahavira

25. Which Indian was the most famous son of Vishwanath Datta and Bhuvaneshwari Devi?
    a) Sri Chaitanya
    b) Sant Kabir
    c) Guru Ram Das
    d) Swami Vivekananda

SCIENCE

1. Whose work on smallpox vaccine was inspired by Blossom the cow ?
   a) Alexander Fleming
   b) Louis Pasteur
   c) Edward Jenner
   d) Alexander Graham Bell

2. Which of these boils at around 2,966° centigrade and melts at around 1,063° centigrade?
   a) Chicken egg
   b) Gold
   c) Chocolate
   d) Apple

3. What became the first successful chemical compound to treat malaria?
   a) Quinine
   b) Penicillin
   c) Petroleum jelly
   d) Neem oil

4. Which part of the human body contains about one hundred million photoreceptors?
   a) Tongue
   b) Nose
   c) Eye
   d) Ear

5. Who, amongst the following, was the nephew of C.V. Raman?
   a) Har Gobind Khorana
   b) S. Chandrasekhar
   c) Homi Bhabha
   d) Jagadish Chandra Bose

6. Which organ of the human body is the pacemaker associated with?
   a) Ear
   b) Heart
   c) Kidney
   d) Small intestine

7. In which category have both Marie Curie and Irene Curie won the Nobel Prize?
   a) Medicine
   b) Literature
   c) Peace
   d) Chemistry

8. The element with the chemical symbol 'Es' is named after …?
   a) Albert Einstein

b) Thomas Alva Edison
c) Ernest Rutherford
d) Ernest Hemingway

9. Hepatic diseases are also called...
   a) Kidney diseases
   b) Heart diseases
   c) Liver diseases
   d) Lung diseases

10. Liberty, Equality and Fraternity are the arcs of a ring of this planet...
    a) Mercury
    b) Venus
    c) Neptune
    d) Saturn

11. Which of these is an output device for a computer?
    a) Digital camera
    b) Mouse
    c) Keyboard
    d) LCD

12. What did Leonardo da Vinci design and define as something that would allow a man 'to throw himself down from any great height without suffering any injury'?
    a) Helicopter
    b) Aeroplane
    c) Parachute
    d) Harness

13. According to the US National Library of Medicine, which is the second-most common disorder, after common cold?
    a) Tooth decay
    b) Cataract
    c) Pneumonia
    d) Headache

14. Which instrument's name comes from two Greek words meaning 'chest', and 'to explore'?
    a) Stethoscope
    b) Barometer
    c) Thermometer
    d) Pacemaker

15. Humphry Davy researched a 'substance X' whose properties were similar to chlorine. What was 'substance X' later known as?
    a) Bromine
    b) Iodine
    c) Carbon
    d) Oxygen

16. In 1696, who became the Warden of the Royal Mint of Great Britain?
    a) Archimedes
    b) Charles Darwin
    c) Isaac Newton
    d) Alfred Nobel

17. Which of these combinations is used to save a document in MS Word?
    a) Ctrl + F
    b) Ctrl + S
    c) Ctrl + Alt
    d) Ctrl + Del

18. Where in the human body would you locate a hammer, an anvil and a stirrup?
    a) Eye
    b) Ear
    c) Nose
    d) Tongue

19. Who among these artists is credited with designing a revolving crane, a pulley, a lagoon dredge and a flying ship?
    a) Leonardo da Vinci
    b) Pablo Picasso
    c) Salvador Dali
    d) Vincent van Gogh

20. What is referred to as a 'hanging monkey' with reference to computers in Germany?
    a) Mouse
    b) Dollar sign
    c) Hard disk
    d) The @ sign

21. Which is the most commonly transplanted organ in the human body?
    a) Liver

b) Ear

c) Kidney

d) Lung

22. What name was chosen by its inventor over Mesh and The Information Mine?

a) Laptop

b) Malware

c) Mouse

d) World Wide Web

23. What did Sir Percy L. Spencer invent following the accidental melting of a chocolate?

a) Pressure cooker

b) Microwave oven

c) Refrigerator

d) Vacuum cleaner

24. Which ancient branch of Indian medicine means 'Knowledge of Life' in Sanskrit?

a) Ayurveda

b) Homeopathy

c) Reiki

d) Acupuncture

25. Which famous Indian's first book was titled *Molecular Diffraction of Light*?

a) A.P.J. Abdul Kalam

b) C.V. Raman

c) Har Gobind Khorana

d) Vikram Sarabhai

GEOGRAPHY

1. Khardung La, Zoji La and Jelep La are names of different…
   a) Lakes in Goa
   b) Mountain passes
   c) Deserts in India
   d) Districts of Kerala

2. In Japan, Goraiko is a special name for…
   a) The sunrise seen from Mount Fuji
   b) The tea used in tea ceremony
   c) The longest river
   d) The best samurai

3. In which state of India is the city of Tezpur?
   a) Bihar
   b) Assam
   c) Chhattisgarh
   d) Odisha

4. Which is the tallest free-standing mountain in the world?
   a) Everest

  b) Kilimanjaro
  c) Fuji
  d) Kanchenjunga

5. Which city connects the Kumbh Mela and Anand
   Bhavan, the home of the Nehrus?
   a) Nashik
   b) Allahabad
   c) Ujjain
   d) Mumbai

6. Which country is the UNESCO World Heritage site
   Aapravasi Ghat situated in?
   a) Fiji
   b) Mauritius
   c) Sri Lanka
   d) China

7. After whom has a lake in the Alpenrausch in
   Switzerland been named?
   a) Rajesh Khanna
   b) Amitabh Bachchan
   c) Shah Rukh Khan
   d) Yash Chopra

8. Which monument was built by Aurangzeb's son as a
   tribute to his mother Rabia Durani?
   a) Hawa Mahal
   b) Bibi Ka Maqbara
   c) Bara Imambara
   d) Gol Gumbaz

9. Which is the largest city in Iraq?
   a) Cairo
   b) Baghdad
   c) Mosul
   d) Karbala

10. In which country would you get to see the 'Long Wall of Ten Thousand Li'?
    a) China
    b) Afghanistan
    c) Japan
    d) Thailand

11. Which state of India do the districts of Korea and Bastar fall in?
    a) Chhattisgarh
    b) Jharkhand
    c) Madhya Pradesh
    d) Kerala

12. Princess Konohana Sakuya is worshipped as the supernatural deity of one of the following peaks. Which one is it?
    a) Kilimanjaro
    b) Mount Fuji
    c) Mount Aconcagua
    d) K2

13. Which is the largest westward flowing river of India?
    a) Narmada
    b) Ganga

c) Irrawaddy
d) Godavari

14. Which peak's first aerial survey was made in 1933?
    a) Mount Everest
    b) Mount Fuji
    c) Mount Kilimanjaro
    d) K2

15. In which Indian state is the Biju Patnaik Airport located?
    a) West Bengal
    b) Odisha
    c) Madhya Pradesh
    d) Punjab

16. Which is the southernmost continent in the world?
    a) Antarctica
    b) Europe
    c) Australia
    d) Africa

17. In 1621, which geographical phenomenon did scientist Pierre Gassendi name after the Roman goddess of dawn and the Roman god of the north wind?
    a) Aurora Australis
    b) Aurora Borealis
    c) Oasis
    d) Mirage

18. On which river in Assam is Majuli, a freshwater river island, located?

a) Ganges
b) Krishna
c) Brahmaputra
d) Kaveri

19. In which present-day country would you see the archaeological ruins at Mohenjodaro?
a) Pakistan
b) Sri Lanka
c) Bhutan
d) Nepal

20. The island Mas a Tierra on which Alexander Selkirk was marooned, is now officially known as......
a) West Indies
b) Robinson Crusoe Island
c) Mauritius
d) Gulliver Island

21. With an altitude of 11,942 feet, which is the highest capital city in the world?
a) La Paz
b) Sydney
c) Beijing
d) Brasilia

22. Which Indian river was referred to as Satadru in Rigvedic times?
a) Saraswati
b) Beas
c) Chenab
d) Sutlej

23. Which port city is also home to the Eastern Naval Command of the Indian Navy?
    a) Visakhapatnam
    b) Kandla
    c) Kolkata
    d) Mumbai

24. Which country's administrative centre is Putrajaya?
    a) Cambodia
    b) Malaysia
    c) Australia
    d) Sri Lanka

25. Which of these is a landlocked state?
    a) Kerala
    b) Gujarat
    c) West Bengal
    d) Jharkhand

LANGUAGE AND LITERATURE

1. In English, which of these punctuation marks is symbolised by two dots?
   a) Semi colon
   b) Comma
   c) Exclamation mark
   d) Colon

2. Which of the following is the title of a book about Winston Smith?
   a) *1857*
   b) *1947*
   c) *1984*
   d) *2012*

3. Who was made a prisoner on the island of Lilliput?
   a) Alice
   b) Swami
   c) Gulliver
   d) Robin Hood

4. Which of these words is derived from the Latin word meaning 'more'?
   a) Plus
   b) Minus
   c) Cos
   d) Pi

5. Whose autobiography was originally written in Gujarati as *Sathiya Sodhani*?
   a) Mahatma Gandhi
   b) Jawaharlal Nehru
   c) Swami Vivekananda
   d) Vallabhbhai Patel

6. Whose name is used to describe a moneylender charging high rates of interest?
   a) Hamlet
   b) Shylock
   c) Romeo
   d) Lady Macbeth

7. Which famous person's life forms the central plot of the novel *Queen of Glory*?
   a) Shahnaz Husain
   b) Rani Laxmi Bai
   c) Gayatri Devi
   d) Mother Teresa

8. *Man of Everest*, also published as *Tiger of the Snows*, is the autobiography of...
   a) Tenzing Norgay

b) Edmund Hillary
c) Roald Amundsen
d) Sunita Williams

9. According to Jules Verne's novel *From The Moon Voyage*, which metal 'possesses the whiteness of silver, the indestructibility of gold, the tenacity of iron, the fusibility of copper, the lightness of glass'?
   a) Platinum
   b) Aluminium
   c) Tin
   d) Lead

10. In the *Harry Potter* series of films, what is common to Ralph Fiennes Christian Coulson and Richard Bremmer?
    a) They all played the role of Harry Potter
    b) They all played the role of Ronald Weasley
    c) They all played the role of Lord Voldemort
    d) They all played the role of Albus Dumbledore

11. In *Alice's Adventures in Wonderland*, who is the only character whom Alice interacts with outside of Wonderland?
    a) The Mad Hatter
    b) The Queen of Hearts
    c) The Cheshire Cat
    d) Alice's sister

12. Which term comes from a medieval Latin word meaning 'manual or book of words'?
    a) Calendar
    b) Dictionary
    c) Atlas
    d) Directory

13. In Shakespeare's *The Merchant of Venice*, if Antonio failed to repay his loan to Shylock, he would have to give...
    a) A dozen diamonds
    b) A pound of his flesh
    c) A pound's worth of silk
    d) A million pounds

14. Who eats a cake marked 'Eat Me' which causes her to grow really tall?
    a) Alice
    b) Thumbelina
    c) Rapunzel
    d) Cheshire Cat

15. What kind of place is Azkaban in the *Harry Potter* series of books?
    a) A prison
    b) A bank
    c) A school
    d) A wand shop

16. Which film director designed the covers of the Bengali translation of Jim Corbett's *Man-Eaters of Kumaon*

and the first edition of Jawaharlal Nehru's *The Discovery of India*?
a) Rabindranath Tagore
b) Ravi Shankar
c) R.K. Laxman
d) Satyajit Ray

17. About which famous author did Leo Tolstoy write: 'I remember the astonishment I felt when I first read _____ ... not only did I feel no delight, but I felt an irresistible repulsion and tedium...'
a) Karl Marx
b) William Shakespeare
c) Rudyard Kipling
d) Charles Dickens

18. Which famous novel begins with the line: 'It was the best of times, it was the worst of times...'?
a) *War and Peace*
b) *Alice's Adventures in Wonderland*
c) *The Adventures of Huckleberry Finn*
d) *A Tale of Two Cities*

19. Which is the official and most widely spoken language of Brazil?
a) Italian
b) Portuguese
c) Arabic
d) German

20. Which of these films is loosely based on Chetan Bhagat's book *Five Point Someone*?
    a) *Munnabhai M.B.B.S.*
    b) *3 Idiots*
    c) *Patiala House*
    d) *Lagaan*

21. Which of these works was first published in a children's magazine as *The Sea-Cook*?
    a) *Alice's Adventures in Wonderland*
    b) *Treasure Island*
    c) *The Adventures of Huckleberry Finn*
    d) *Gulliver's Travels*

22. In *Asterix* comics, who could make beautiful flowers grow in moments?
    a) Getafix
    b) Botanix
    c) Prefix
    d) Suffix

23. With which comic-strip character would you associate Gwen Stacy?
    a) Spider-Man
    b) Superman
    c) Batman
    d) Phantom

24. Which of these was known in Europe as *The Fables of Bidpai*?
    a) Panchatantra

b) Bhagvad Gita
c)One Thousand and One Nights
d) Mahabharata

25. Of all these characters created by William Shakespeare, who has the most lines to deliver?
a) Lady Macbeth
b) Hamlet
c) Othello
d) Romeo

POLITICS

1. In 1984, who was rated as the world's 'Best Finance Minister' by *Euromoney* magazine?
   a) R. Venkataraman
   b) Manmohan Singh
   c) Pranab Mukherjee
   d) Yashwant Sinha

2. What came down in India on 28 March 1989, from twenty-one to eighteen?
   a) The number of states in India
   b) Voting age
   c) The number of cases of chickenpox
   d) National holidays

3. Which country's first woman prime minister was Khaleda Zia?
   a) Pakistan
   b) Sri Lanka
   c) Bangladesh
   d) Indonesia

4. In India, which ministry provides passports for citizens?
   a) Ministry of Railways
   b) Ministry of Textiles
   c) Ministry of Civil Aviation
   d) Ministry of External Affairs

5. Before the Supreme Court of India moved to its present building, where did it function from?
   a) Parliament House
   b) Rashtrapati Bhavan
   c) Red Fort
   d) Charminar

6. Which yesteryear Indian politician was nominated five times for the Nobel Prize in Literature from 1933 to 1937?
   a) Jawaharlal Nehru
   b) C. Rajagopalachari
   c) S. Radhakrishnan
   d) Atal Bihari Vajpayee

7. Who was the last governor-general of independent India?
   a) C. Rajagopalachari
   b) Rajendra Prasad
   c) Jawaharlal Nehru
   d) B.R. Ambedkar

8. Who has been the only woman finance minister of
   India so far?
   a) Indira Gandhi
   b) Meira Kumar
   c) Pratibha Patil
   d) Kiran Bedi

9. Who was named 'Person of the Year' in 2012 by *Time*
   magazine?
   a) Barack Obama
   b) Angela Merkel
   c) Usain Bolt
   d) David Cameron

10. Which leader's autobiography is *Toward Freedom*?
    a) Bal Gangadhar Tilak
    b) Vallabhbhai Patel
    c) Maulana Abul Kalam Azad
    d) Jawaharlal Nehru

11. In 2004, Hamid Karzai became the first
    democratically elected president of which country?
    a) Pakistan
    b) Indonesia
    c) Afghanistan
    d) Bangladesh

12. Which leader's sister was the first Indian woman to
    hold a cabinet portfolio?
    a) Manmohan Singh
    b) Jawaharlal Nehru

c) B.R. Ambedkar
d) A.P.J. Abdul Kalam

13. Where is Sheikh Mujibur Rahman regarded as the
    'Father of the Nation'?
    a) Pakistan
    b) Bangladesh
    c) Bahrain
    d) Kuwait

14. Who was the first vice-president of India to become
    president?
    a) Rajendra Prasad
    b) S. Radhakrishnan
    c) V.V. Giri
    d) N. Sanjiva Reddy

15. Who is the first African American to hold the office of
    the president of the USA?
    a) Thomas Jefferson
    b) John F. Kennedy
    c) Barack Obama
    d) George Washington

16. Which of these countries had rulers primarily
    addressed by the title of 'Czar'?
    a) Spain
    b) Germany
    c) Japan
    d) Russia

17. Which finance minister had the opportunity to present two budgets on his birthday – in 1964 and 1968?
    a) Jawaharlal Nehru
    b) Rajiv Gandhi
    c) Morarji Desai
    d) Manmohan Singh

18. Which of these is the samadhi sthal (memorial ground) of Jawaharlal Nehru?
    a) Shanti Van
    b) Vijay Ghat
    c) Shakti Sthal
    d) Kisan Ghat

19. Who assumed the twin titles of Fuhrer and Chancellor of Germany after Paul von Hindenburg's death?
    a) Winston Churchill
    b) Adolf Hitler
    c) Abraham Lincoln
    d) Benito Mussolini

20. Who was the first Indian woman ambassador to the USSR?
    a) Indira Gandhi
    b) Sarojini Naidu
    c) Annie Besant
    d) Vijaya Lakshmi Pandit

21. Who was awarded the Nobel Peace Prize in 1991 but gave the acceptance speech in 2012?
    a) Nelson Mandela

b) Aung San Suu Kyi

c) Amartya Sen

d) Angela Merkel

22. Till date, who has been the youngest prime minister of India?
   a) Lal Bahadur Shastri
   b) Chaudhary Charan Singh
   c) Morarji Desai
   d) Rajiv Gandhi

23. After which of these wars was the League of Nations formed?
   a) World War I
   b) World War II
   c) Gulf War
   d) Vietnam War

24. Which country's monarch is known as the 'Druk Gyalpo' or 'Dragon King'?
   a) Sri Lanka
   b) Bhutan
   c) Nepal
   d) Myanmar

25. Who voted for the first time in life on 27 April 1994, at the age of seventy-five?
   a) Dalai Lama
   b) Nelson Mandela
   c) Mother Teresa
   d) Bill Clinton

ENTERTAINMENT

1. In a textbook, the chapter titled *From Bus Conductor To Superstar*, is based on which of the following?
   a) M.G. Ramachandran
   b) Rajinikanth
   c) M.S. Swaminathan
   d) Gundappa Viswanath

2. Which of these did not feature a real life father-son as father-son in the film?
   a) *Yamla Pagla Deewana*
   b) *Sarkar*
   c) *Munnabhai M.B.B.S.*
   d) *Bunty Aur Babli*

3. Which of these is generally held with one hand and played with the other?
   a) Tabla
   b) Xylophone
   c) Mridangam
   d) Duffli

4. Which actor was only six years old when he appeared
    in his first film *Aasha*?
    a) Saif Ali Khan
    b) Salman Khan
    c) Hrithik Roshan
    d) Aamir Khan

5. Which of these superheroes was found on the
    Bengalla coast?
    a) Superman
    b) Phantom
    c) Batman
    d) Spider-Man

6. Abdul Rashid Salim are part of which actor's full
    name?
    a) Aamir Khan
    b) Shah Rukh Khan
    c) Irrfan Khan
    d) Salman Khan

7. According to Google, which was the most searched
    Indian film in 2012?
    a) *Jannat 2*
    b) *Kahaani*
    c) *Ek Tha Tiger*
    d) *Agent Vinod*

8. In the *Tom and Jerry* cartoons, what kind of a creature
    is Spike?
    a) Cat

b) Dog
c) Fox
d) Wolf

9. Which maestro taught George Harrison to play the sitar?
a) Norah Jones
b) Anoushka Shankar
c) Ravi Shankar
d) Zakir Hussain

10. Morty and Ferdy are this famous cartoon character's nephews. Who is he?
a) Popeye
b) Donald Duck
c) Henry
d) Mickey Mouse

11. Which famous Hindi film actor is the grandson of the well known Urdu poet Harivansh Rai Srivastav?
a) Amitabh Bachchan
b) Shah Rukh Khan
c) Saif Ali Khan
d) Abhishek Bachchan

12. Who is the famous husband of actress Genelia D'souza?
a) Saif Ali Khan
b) Riteish Deshmukh
c) Imran Khan
d) Ranveer Singh

13. I am a lazy fat cat who hates Mondays, loves lasagna, and my owner is Jon Arbuckle. Which cartoon character am I?
    a) Crookshanks
    b) Garfield
    c) Tom
    d) Cheshire Cat

14. Which famous film's name was suggested by Kirron Kher?
    a) *Dilwale Dulhania Le Jayenge*
    b) *Ra.One*
    c) *Taare Zameen Par*
    d) *Kai Po Che!*

15. Who played the role of Imraan in the 2011 film *Zindagi Na Milegi Dobara*?
    a) Farhan Akhtar
    b) Hrithik Roshan
    c) Abhay Deol
    d) Saif Ali Khan

16. Who sang as a playback singer in the 1956 film *Basant Bahar*?
    a) Ravi Shankar
    b) M.S. Subbulakshmi
    c) Bhimsen Joshi
    d) Zakir Hussain

17. Name the pet tiger of the cartoon character Calvin.
    a) Hobbes

    b) Ruff

    c) Hot Dog

    d) Snoopy

18. Among these actors, which one has represented India in rugby?
    a) Aamir Khan
    b) Rahul Bose
    c) Farhan Akhtar
    d) Abhishek Bachchan

19. Which of these actor's first English language film was *The Last Lear*?
    a) Amitabh Bachchan
    b) Irrfan Khan
    c) Naseeruddin Shah
    d) Om Puri

20. Who was the director of the 2013 film *Vishwaroopam*?
    a) Prakash Raj
    b) Rohit Shetty
    c) Rajnikanth
    d) Kamal Haasan

21. Who received the Dadasaheb Phalke Award in 2007?
    a) Shyam Benegal
    b) Manna Dey
    c) Mrinal Sen
    d) Asha Bhosle

22. Who returned to the silver screen after fourteen years with the film *English Vinglish*?

a) Karisma Kapoor
b) Sridevi
c) Juhi Chawla
d) Madhuri Dixit

23. Who played the female lead in the films *Delhi-6, Aisha*
and *Saawariya*?
a) Sonam Kapoor
b) Deepika Padukone
c) Priyanka Chopra
d) Amrita Rao

24. Which comic strip character has a brain that works
faster than a computer?
a) Chacha Chaudhary
b) Suppandi
c) Pavithra Prabhakar
d) Shaktimaan

25. Which was Salman Khan and Katrina Kaif's first film
together?
a) *Maine Pyar Kyun Kiya*
b) *Ek Tha Tiger*
c) *Rajneeti*
d) *Race*

SPORTS

1. Among Indians, who has scored the most runs from fours and sixes in a single Test innings?
   a) M. S. Dhoni
   b) Virender Sehwag
   c) Sachin Tendulkar
   d) Sourav Ganguly

2. Which sport is the term 'silly point' associated with?
   a) Kho Kho
   b) Cricket
   c) Kabaddi
   d) Football

3. Which lady's autobiography is titled *Playing To Win* ?
   a) Sania Mirza
   b) P.T. Usha
   c) Jhulan Goswami
   d) Saina Nehwal

4. In the history of the FIFA World Cup, Lucien Laurent of France was the first player to...
   a) Be red-carded

b) Be substituted
c) Score a goal
d) Referee a match

5. In an international football match, if a player is in his own half, which of these is true?
a) Can handle the ball
b) Can stop a player with hand
c) Cannot be ruled offside
d) Cannot be red-carded

6. The English Premier League started in 1992-93. Which team won it in that inaugural year?
a) Manchester United
b) Newcastle United
c) Arsenal
d) Blackburn Rovers

7. Of these teams, which one has played the least number of Test matches?
a) Australia
b) Zimbabwe
c) India
d) Pakistan

8. Who wrote a book titled *The Jubilee Book of Cricket*?
a) Ranjitsinhji
b) Dhyan Chand
c) Dhanraj Pillai
d) Milkha Singh

9. After Sachin Tendulkar, who has scored the most runs in Test cricket?
   a) S. Chanderpaul
   b) Virender Sehwag
   c) Ricky Ponting
   d) K. Sangakkara

10. How many times has India won the ICC Cricket World Cup?
    a) Once
    b) Twice
    c) Thrice
    d) Six times

11. Which city's IPL team bears the name 'Sunrisers'?
    a) Bengaluru
    b) Hyderabad
    c) Chennai
    d) Kolkata

12. Which team has played the most number of one-day internationals?
    a) India
    b) New Zealand
    c) Pakistan
    d) England

13. Who holds the record for the most number of dismissals as a wicketkeeper in Test cricket?
    a) Adam Gilchrist
    b) Ian Healy

c) M.S. Dhoni

d) Mark Boucher

14. In ODIs, which team has scored four hundred-plus runs in a match, the most number of times?
    a) Sri Lanka
    b) India
    c) South Africa
    d) New Zealand

15. Excluding friendlies, who has scored the most number of goals for FC Barcelona in all competitions?
    a) Ronaldinho
    b) Lionel Messi
    c) Neymar
    d) Cesc Fabregas

16. In Test cricket, which is the only team to have lost five wickets for no run in a Test innings thrice?
    a) India
    b) Bangladesh
    c) New Zealand
    d) Pakistan

17. Which Olympic sport takes place on a mat called 'tatami', with the contest lasting five minutes?
    a) Karate
    b) Judo
    c) Boxing
    d) Wrestling

18. Who is the highest scoring captain of India in ODIs?
    a) Sourav Ganguly
    b) Mohammad Azharuddin
    c) Sachin Tendulkar
    d) M.S. Dhoni

19. At the London Olympics of 1908, the distance from Windsor Castle to the Royal Box in the Olympic Stadium was fixed for this event.
    a) Triathlon
    b) Marathon
    c) Sailing
    d) Dressage

20. Apart from Rohan Gavaskar, which other cricketer's father has also played ODIs for India?
    a) M.S. Dhoni
    b) Yuvraj Singh
    c) Virender Sehwag
    d) Sachin Tendulkar

21. In cricket, what is a 'Golden Duck'?
    a) When a batsman is out on a duck in the second innings of a Test
    b) When a batsman is out on the first ball he faces
    c) When a batsman scores 0 in both innings of a Test
    d) When a batsman remains unbeaten on 0

22. In Twenty20 Internationals, who has hit the most number of sixes in his career?
    a) Yuvraj Singh

b) Kevin Pietersen
c) Brendon McCullum
d) Chris Gayle

23. Ken Aston, a football referee, was inspired by traffic lights to start one of the following.
    a) Yellow and red cards
    b) Different coloured jerseys
    c) Red and green footballs
    d) Colour of flags

24. Hook, Jab and Uppercut are techniques used in this sport. Name it!
    a) Boxing
    b) Shooting
    c) Karate
    d) Judo

25. In 1920, a two-member squad of P.C. Banerjee and P.F. Chaugle represented India at the Olympic Games. In which discipline did they perform?
    a) Athletics
    b) Swimming
    c) Gymnastics
    d) Wrestling

RELIGION AND MYTHOLOGY

1. Whose first sermon is called Dharmachakra Pravartana Sutra?
   a) Mahavira
   b) Buddha
   c) Guru Nanak
   d) Shankaracharya

2. In Hindu mythology, who balanced the Govardhana mountain on his finger to protect his people from Indra's wrath?
   a) Krishna
   b) Rama
   c) Bharata
   d) Parashurama

3. In Hindu mythology, who was also known as Dasanana as he had ten faces?
   a) Rama
   b) Hanuman
   c) Ravana
   d) Garuda

4. With which religion would you associate the 'Guru ka Langar'?
    a) Hinduism
    b) Christianity
    c) Sikhism
    d) Buddhism

5. In the Mahabharata, who was Kunti's eldest son?
    a) Arjuna
    b) Karna
    c) Yudhishthira
    d) Nakula

6. Which character from the Ramayana was given his name by the devas due to a scar inflicted on his jaw by Indra's vajra?
    a) Sugriva
    b) Bali
    c) Hanuman
    d) Ravana

7. In the Mahabharata, which modern-day city in India was known as Indraprastha, where the Pandavas lived?
    a) Calcutta
    b) Bombay
    c) Delhi
    d) Hyderabad

8. Which was the first Sanskrit work chosen for English translation by the Asiatic Society?
   a) Mahabharata
   b) Ramayana
   c) Abhijnanasakuntalam
   d) Jataka Tales

9. Which character's name in the Ramayana literally means 'furrow', as she was found by her father while he was ploughing the field?
   a) Urmila
   b) Sita
   c) Mandodari
   d) Mandavi

10. In Hinduism, the spots on the peacock's tail symbolize the...
    a) Eyes of the gods
    b) Shiva's trishul
    c) Krishna's footprints
    d) Hanuman's teardrops

11. Which Hindu god's divine bow is Pinaka, the multi-barrel rocket launcher developed for the Indian Army, named after?
    a) Rama
    b) Lakshmana
    c) Shiva
    d) Krishna

12. Which Indian literary work has been retold by Kamban in Tamil, Madhava Kandali in Assamese and Krittibas Ojha in Bengali?
   a) Mahabharata
   b) Ramayana
   c) Jataka Tales
   d) Meghadutta

13. According to the Mahabharata, who among these was Shakuni's sister?
   a) Uttara
   b) Draupadi
   c) Gandhari
   d) Kunti

14. In Hindu mythology, which god wrote the Mahabharata to Vyasa's dictation?
   a) Hanuman
   b) Ganesha
   c) Shiva
   d) Krishna

15. According to Hindu mythology, from which part of Brahma's body was the sage Narada born?
   a) Ear
   b) Toe
   c) Thumb
   d) Lap

16. In Hindu mythology, whose devotee was Prahlada?
   a) Vishnu

b) Brahma

c) Shiva

d) Indra

17. According to Hindu mythology, which god is the creator of the universe?
    a) Shiva
    b) Indra
    c) Vishnu
    d) Brahma

18. With which religion would you associate a 'nihang'?
    a) Sikhism
    b) Taoism
    c) Jainism
    d) Zoroastrianism

19. As per Hindu mythology, who constructed the city of Lanka?
    a) Vishwakarma
    b) Sushruta
    c) Dhanvantari
    d) Narada

20. Who was Dashratha's first wife?
    a) Kaushalya
    b) Kaikeyi
    c) Madri
    d) Sumitra

21. In Hinduism, whose form did Vishnu assume to divide the Vedas into four different parts?

a) Valmiki
b) Veda Vyasa
c) Tulsidas
d) Vishnu Sharma

22. In the Ramayana, 'venu', 'mridang', 'dundubhi' and 'shankha' were names of...
a) Sita's sisters
b) Musical instruments
c) Chapters
d) Arjuna's bows

23. Which religion was introduced in Bhutan by the Indian guru Padmasambhava?
a) Buddhism
b) Jainism
c) Sikhism
d) Christianity

24. In the Mahabharata, who was married to Hidimbi?
a) Bhima
b) Arjuna
c) Nakula
d) Sahadeva

25. According to Hindu mythology, who was the seventh incarnation of Mahavishnu?
a) Krishna
b) Rama
c) Vamana
d) Narasimha

NATURE AND WILDLIFE

1. At about six feet, which animal's legs are taller than many human beings?
   a) Zebra
   b) Hippopotamus
   c) Giraffe
   d) Bulldog

2. Which country is home to nine out of ten of the world's orangutans?
   a) China
   b) Indonesia
   c) Kenya
   d) South Africa

3. Which animal is the source of the vast majority of human rabies cases?
   a) Cow
   b) Sheep
   c) Cat
   d) Dog

4. Which fibre is produced from the plants of the genus *Gossypium*?
   a) Mohair
   b) Jute
   c) Cotton
   d) Wool

5. Black mambas get their name from the blue-black colour of their...
   a) Pupils
   b) Skin
   c) Insides of the mouth
   d) Fangs

6. What makes the African pygmy squirrel special?
   a) It is the smallest squirrel
   b) It is the heaviest squirrel
   c) It is the largest squirrel
   d) It is the largest mammal

7. Which are the only known mammals that survive solely on blood?
   a) Polar bears
   b) Asiatic lions
   c) Vampire bats
   d) Dog fleas

8. Which of the following do not lay eggs?
   a) Mosquitoes
   b) Penguins
   c) King cobras
   d) Kangaroos

9. Which of the following owes its name to the tree's Quechua name meaning 'bark of barks'?
    a) Cardamom
    b) Quinine
    c) Nutmeg
    d) Penicillin

10. Which is the largest snake in the world, when both weight and length are considered?
    a) Rattlesnake
    b) King cobra
    c) Black mamba
    d) Green anaconda

11. Its natural habitat is only in a small part of China and the Chinese name for this animal translates to 'large bear-cat'? Which one of the following is it?
    a) Porcupine
    b) Raccoon
    c) Giant panda
    d) Koala

12. In which state is the Khangchendzonga National Park located?
    a) Sikkim
    b) Goa
    c) Tamil Nadu
    d) Uttar Pradesh

13. The name hummingbird comes from...
    a) The bird's call

b) The sound made by its wings

c) The flower it visits

d) The place of its origin

14. Which bird's eggs are the largest in relation to its body size?
    a) Ostrich
    b) Eagle
    c) Pigeon
    d) Kiwi

15. Which member of the cat family appears on the state emblem of India?
    a) Tiger
    b) Cheetah
    c) Lion
    d) Puma

16. What is the name of Joy Adamson's first novel based on the life of a lion cub?
    a) Pippa's Challenge
    b) Born Free
    c) The Searching Spirit
    d) Queen of Sheba

17. Which mammal's name owes its origins to a Greek word meaning 'a fish with a womb'?
    a) Octopus
    b) Shark
    c) Blue whale
    d) Dolphin

18. Which part of an enemy's body does the spitting cobra of Africa aim at?
    a) Eyes
    b) Neck
    c) Feet
    d) Ears

19. Which of the following make up a quarter of all mammals?
    a) Bats
    b) Bears
    c) Elephants
    d) Orangutans

20. Which animal's name comes from the Sanskrit word *chitraka* meaning 'the spotted one'?
    a) Chital
    b) Cheetah
    c) Caribou
    d) Crocodile

21. Which bird from the sword-billed species has the longest bill of any bird relative to its body length?
    a) Crane
    b) Kingfisher
    c) Pelican
    d) Hummingbird

22. Which country is home to the Sagarmatha National Park?
    a) India

b) Sri Lanka
c) Bhutan
d) Nepal

23. Which of these creatures has a species known as 'turban shell'?
    a) Crab
    b) Tortoise
    c) Oyster
    d) Snail

24. Which tree appears on the emblem of Saudi Arabia?
    a) Date palm
    b) Coconut
    c) Neem
    d) Mango

25. Which is the only bird to have its nose at the end of its bill?
    a) Kingfisher
    b) Kiwi
    c) Crow
    d) Pelican

ART AND CULTURE

1. Traditionally, chikankari was done on white cloth with threads of this colour. Name the colour.
   a) White
   b) Red
   c) Orange
   d) Green

2. What is known as *kolam* in Tamil Nadu, *mandana* in Rajasthan and *aripana* in Bihar?
   a) Sari
   b) Carpet
   c) Rangoli
   d) Roti

3. Who said this after winning a Grammy: 'I've been appreciated only twice by my guru, Ustad Allah Rakha'?
   a) Bismillah Khan
   b) Amjad Ali Khan
   c) Rashid Khan
   d) Zakir Hussain

4. Which of these theatre forms originated in Kerala?
   a) Nautanki
   b) Koodiyaattam
   c) Bhavai
   d) Bhaona

5. In which state is the Mamallapuram Dance Festival celebrated?
   a) Kerala
   b) Karnataka
   c) Tamil Nadu
   d) Uttar Pradesh

6. Which of these is a knee-length coat buttoning to the neck, worn by men from South Asia?
   a) Sherwani
   b) Mekhala
   c) Poncho
   d) Capri

7. Which of these is a stringed instrument?
   a) Ghatam
   b) Mandolin
   c) Shehnai
   d) Bansuri

8. Who was the music director of All India Radio from 1949 to 1956?
   a) Ravi Shankar
   b) Bismillah Khan
   c) Shiv Kumar Sharma
   d) Zakir Hussain

9. In Jainism, which festival commemorates Mahavira's attainment of 'moksha' or salvation?
   a) Diwali
   b) Holi
   c) Vasant Panchami
   d) Raksha Bandhan

10. Who composed a number of songs and plays under the pen name 'Akhtari Pia'?
   a) Munshi Premchand
   b) Nawab Wajid Ali Shah
   c) Tansen
   d) Akbar

11. In which part of the human body is a 'jhanjhar' worn?
   a) Neck
   b) Ear
   c) Wrist
   d) Ankle

12. Which of these dance forms developed in Tamil Nadu?
   a) Kathak
   b) Bharatanatyam
   c) Kuchipudi
   d) Odissi

13. Which musician's official website is called 'sarod. com'?
   a) Zakir Hussain
   b) Ravi Shankar

c) Amjad Ali Khan
d) Ali Akbar Khan

14. Which state is known for the martial art form Kalaripayattu?
a) Tamil Nadu
b) Kerala
c) Karnataka
d) Maharashtra

15. According to legend, the Tarnetar Mela in Gujarat coincides with their wedding celebrations at the Trineteshwar Temple. Who are they?
a) Arjuna and Draupadi
b) Ram and Sita
c) Radha and Krishna
d) Nala and Damayanti

16. With which country would you associate ikebana, the art of flower arrangement?
a) Japan
b) Germany
c) Nepal
d) Thailand

17. Which musician of India forms the basis of the book *Abba... God's Greatest Gift to Us*?
a) Bismillah Khan
b) Amjad Ali Khan
c) Rashid Khan
d) Zakir Hussain

18. Which of these festivals is normally celebrated in the month of 'Phalguna'?
    a) Diwali
    b) Holi
    c) Dussehra
    d) Raksha Bandhan

19. In 1970, who went to the United States and performed his first concert at the Fillmore East in New York City with Pandit Ravi Shankar?
    a) Bismillah Khan
    b) Amjad Ali Khan
    c) Rashid Khan
    d) Zakir Hussain

20. Which of these states would you associate patola weaving with?
    a) Gujarat
    b) West Bengal
    c) Jammu and Kashmir
    d) Nagaland

21. In Madhya Pradesh, Tansen Samman is the highest award in which field?
    a) Classical music
    b) Literature
    c) Sports
    d) Physics

22. Whom did Nand Das base his initial plays of the Rasleela on?

a) Rama
b) Krishna
c) Hanuman
d) Arjuna

23. In Indian music, what is the term given to the first line of a song or composition?
    a) Mukhda
    b) Sargam
    c) Taal
    d) Antara

24. Who was named the Best Worldbeat Drummer by *Drum* magazine in 2007?
    a) Ravi Shankar
    b) Allah Rakha Khan
    c) Amjad Ali Khan
    d) Zakir Hussain

25. The book, *Bapi... The Love of my Life*, is a daughter's tribute to...
    a) M.F. Hussain
    b) Shatrughan Sinha
    c) Ravi Shankar
    d) Pranab Mukherjee

FOOD

1. Which country is known for the Cantonese and Szechwan cooking styles?
   a) Japan
   b) China
   c) Italy
   d) Portugal

2. *Citrus reticulata* is the most important commercial species of what in India?
   a) Apple
   b) Mango
   c) Banana
   d) Orange

3. Who is regarded as the 'Father of White Revolution' in India?
   a) Sundarlal Bahuguna
   b) Baba Amte
   c) V. Kurien
   d) M. S. Swaminathan

4. Which of these sweets is similar to a lalmohan?

a) Jalebi
b) Gulab jamun
c) Petha
d) Rabri

5. What was known by names such as 'gola' and 'satha' in the eighteenth century?
   a) Onion
   b) Potato
   c) Cauliflower
   d) Radish

6. Which is the most commonly eaten part of a carrot plant?
   a) Root
   b) Leaf
   c) Branch
   d) Flower

7. Which state is the largest producer of apples in India?
   a) Rajasthan
   b) Jammu and Kashmir
   c) Jharkhand
   d) Tamil Nadu

8. Which of these is a ball of deep-fried paneer boiled in sugar syrup?
   a) Gajar halwa
   b) Gulab jamun
   c) Shrikhand
   d) Kulfi

9. In 1877, what was first produced in Bikaner during the
   reign of Maharaja Dungar Singh?
   a) Rasgulla
   b) Bhujia
   c) Idli
   d) Thekua

10. Ranbir, Taraori, Kasturi and Mahi Sugandha are types
    of...
    a) Basmati rice
    b) Darjeeling tea
    c) Rasgullas
    d) Motichoor laddoos

11. What is the most common method of potato
    preparation across the world?
    a) Boiling
    b) Deep frying
    c) Pickling
    d) Mashing

12. Which spice, known as *zanjabil* in Arabic, is the dried
    underground stem of a herbaceous tropical plant?
    a) Garlic
    b) Ginger
    c) Chilli
    d) Coriander

13. The recipe of 'Jahangiri', a sweet, is believed to be
    listed in Al Baghdadi's cookery book of the thirteenth
    century. How do we know it better?

a) Kulfi
b) Jalebi
c) Gulab jamun
d) Barfi

14. What are Trinidad Scorpion Butch T, Bhut Jolokia and Naga Viper varieties of?
    a) Scorpions
    b) Chillies
    c) Stamps
    d) Tea

15. Which spice is the dried unopened bud of *Syzygium aromaticum*?
    a) Cardamom
    b) Cinnamon
    c) Clove
    d) Nutmeg

16. In which state does the 'Vasta Waza' supervise a special thirty-six course meal known as the 'Wazvan'?
    a) Jammu and Kashmir
    b) Uttar Pradesh
    c) Tamil Nadu
    d) Karnataka

17. In 2011, this food was named as the world's most popular dish in a global survey conducted by the charity Oxfam. Name it.
    a) Sandwich
    b) Biscuit

c) Pasta

d) Pizza

18. Which of these is normally produced by freezing it in small containers?

a) Rasgulla

b) Kulfi

c) Jalebi

d) Petha

19. The famous layered dessert 'Bebinca', made of flour, coconut milk and eggs in a clay oven, is a speciality of this state in India. Name the state.

a) Goa

b) Karnataka

c) Nagaland

d) Punjab

20. Which food item was used before erasers to erase pencil marks?

a) Bread crumbs

b) Salt

c) Wheat dough

d) Rice

21. In the poem *Johnny Johnny...*, what was Johnny eating?

a) Sugar

b) Chocolate

c) Apple

d) Orange

22. Which of these sweets is also the name of a film directed by Anurag Basu?
    a) Rasgulla
    b) Laddoo
    c) Barfi
    d) Sandesh

23. What comes in two basic shapes: snowflake and mushroom?
    a) Pasta
    b) Cake
    c) Ice cream
    d) Popped popcorn

24. Which fruit has varieties like Allahabad Safeda, Banarasi, Chittidar and Harijha?
    a) Apple
    b) Banana
    c) Orange
    d) Guava

25. Which of these vegetables bears the scientific name of *Solanum tuberosum*?
    a) Carrot
    b) Tomato
    c) Potato
    d) Brinjal

GENERAL

1. Which of the following is not a natural fibre?
    a) Silk
    b) Cotton
    c) Nylon
    d) Jute

2. Which part of the human body does the hill station Nainital gets its name from?
    a) Ears
    b) Eyes
    c) Lips
    d) Feet

3. What is the number of thousand rupee notes you would need in India, to become a crorepati?
    a) Hundred
    b) Thousand
    c) Ten thousand
    d) One lakh

4. If jodhpurs are trousers for horse riding, then what are patialas?
   a) Tea cups
   b) Pleated salwars
   c) Embroidered bags
   d) Painted carpets

5. Which colour is common to the flags of Canada and China?
   a) Green
   b) Red
   c) Blue
   d) Yellow

6. Sherpas are known for their skill in...
   a) Breeding camels
   b) Sword fighting
   c) Mountaineering
   d) Scuba diving

7. If you subtracted hundred lakhs from one crore, what would you be left with?
   a) Nothing
   b) Ten thousand
   c) One lakh
   d) One million

8. Which of these is an eye cosmetic?
   a) Surma
   b) Gajra
   c) Bindi
   d) Kundal

9. Which colour appears between blue and yellow in a
    rainbow?
    a) Red
    b) Green
    c) Orange
    d) Indigo

10. Who among these Nobel laureates was not born in
    India?
    a) Ronald Ross
    b) Rudyard Kipling
    c) Mother Teresa
    d) Amartya Sen

11. The writer Washington Irving was the first person to
    describe that Father Christmas or Santa Claus...
    a) Wears a red outfit
    b) Slides down chimneys
    c) Owns Rudolph the reindeer
    d) Lives in London

12. Weighing just 0.03 grams, Treskilling Yellow is
    thought to be the most valuable thing in existence by
    weight and volume. What is it?
    a) A stamp
    b) A needle
    c) A coin
    d) A nail

13. Which object on the new flag of Bhutan was first
    painted by Kilkhor Lopen Jada?

a) The dragon
b) The lion
c) The maple leaf
d) The star

14. In Venice, a gondola is a type of…
    a) Boat
    b) Stringed instrument
    c) Sweet
    d) Paper

15. In India, which profession would you pursue with an LLB degree?
    a) Medicine
    b) Law
    c) Architecture
    d) Quizzing

16. Which word meaning 'celestial announcement' was coined in 1935, in the rented house of a professor, M.V. Gopalaswamy?
    a) Inquilab Zindabad
    b) Akashvani
    c) Jai Hind
    d) Vande Mataram

17. Which colour is common to the flags of Bangladesh, Switzerland and Japan?
    a) Green
    b) Red
    c) Orange
    d) White

18. Which precious stone owes its origins to the Latin word for 'seawater'?
    a) Turquoise
    b) Aquamarine
    c) Emerald
    d) Topaz

19. In 1937, Crystal City in Texas erected a statue to honor E. C. Segar and Popeye for their...
    a) Positive influence on America's eating habits
    b) Contribution to environment awareness
    c) Role in developing reading habits
    d) Role in developing sleeping habits

20. Which famous person once said: 'By blood, I am Albanian. By citizenship, an Indian... As to my calling, I belong to the world....'?
    a) Nelson Mandela
    b) Jawaharlal Nehru
    c) Mother Teresa
    d) Mahatma Gandhi

21. According to the Chinese calendar, which animal or reptile was 2013 (starting on 10 February of the Gregorian calendar), the year of?
    a) Snake
    b) Rabbit
    c) Rat
    d) Horse

22. In the 1940s, the map on this flag was redrawn by the cartographer Leo Drozdoff. Which organisation did it stand for?
    a) United Nations
    b) European Union
    c) Bhutan
    d) Sri Lanka

23. Which is the first YouTube video to hit more than one billion likes?
    a) Obama victory speech
    b) Usain Bolt 100 m sprint
    c) Curiosity on Mars
    d) Gangnam Style

24. Which of these is the name of a twelve-digit unique number provided by the Unique Identification Authority of India?
    a) Aadhaar
    b) Suraksha
    c) Nirmaan
    d) Vardaan

25. Which neighbouring country's currency is Kyat?
    a) Myanmar
    b) Sri Lanka
    c) Bangladesh
    d) Pakistan

SUPEROVER

SET 1

1. *Dalchini* is a type of sugar: serious or joking?

2. Which Sanskrit poem's title translates into 'cloud–messenger'?

3. Which species of deer sounds like a dish from southern India?

4. The best preserved part of this UNESCO World Heritage site dates to the Ming dynasty.

5. In 1921, which Nobel Prize winner was given a gram of radium for her service to science?

6. Glen Mills coached which two-time triple Olympic Games gold medallist and world record holder?

SET 2

1. Just like human beings, chimpanzees do not have hair on lips, palms and soles of the feet: serious or joking?

2. In literature, who ended up in a London gang of thieves led by Fagin?

3. Which explorer's smallest ship was Santa Clara, nicknamed Nina (Spanish for 'girl')?

4. Which is the only IPL team that has a number in its name?

5. What was adopted as Japan's official monetary unit in 1871?

6. According to the Gregorian calendar, which national holiday in India is celebrated in the first month?

SET 3

1. Itanagar is named after Ita Fort meaning 'fort of bricks': serious or joking?

2. How many horns does the black rhinoceros have?

3. Who was the first prime minister of India to receive the Bharat Ratna?

4. Which deity's name would you find in the acronym ISKCON?

5. In 2012, who defeated Israel's Boris Gelfand to win the World Chess Championship?

6. Which is heavier: one thousand and fifty gm of cotton or one kg of iron?

SET 4

1. Orangutans live in the wild only in Borneo and northern Sumatra: serious or joking?

2. How do we better know the Baha'i Mashriqu'l-Adhkar in New Delhi?

3. Imran Tahir and Usman Khawaja were both born in Pakistan. If Imran plays for South Africa, which team does Usman play for?

4. Whose address is given as Arctic Circle, 96930 Rovaniemi by the Finnish Tourist Board?

5. Which play by William Shakespeare features the line, 'To be or not to be…'?

6. From which city did the British shift their capital to Delhi in 1911?

SET 5

1. In many churches in Armenia and Serbia, Christmas is celebrated in January: serious or joking?

2. Which Indian city was formerly known as Anandavana, Kashika and Rudravasa?

3. How is the Scottish king Mac Bethad mac Findlaich better known?

4. Over sixty percent of the gold that has been mined is used for making this.

5. What is the symbol of the Samajwadi Party?

6. Which animated character's main rival is the ten-year-old Kalia?

SET 6

1. In the human body, the cornea contains blood: serious or joking?

2. In comics, which creature's bite granted Peter Parker incredible powers?

3. Which fruit is supposed to have inspired Isaac Newton to propound his 'Law of Gravitation'?

4. In which union territory of India would one find the naval base INS Dweeprakshak?

5. The cultivation of grapevines is called...

6. Which country's national anthem is called 'The Thunder Dragon Kingdom'?

SET 7

1. Starfish have no brains: serious or joking?

2. Which actress's nickname is Bebo?

3. If Babur was the first emperor of this dynasty, who was the last?

4. In a game of chess, which is the only piece that cannot retreat?

5. What replaced the king's portrait on the currency of Nepal in 2007?

6. In Hindu mythology, who is also known as Bajrang Bali?

SET 8

1. In India, all letter boxes are red in colour: serious or joking?

2. 'An eye for an eye only ends up making the whole world _____'. Fill in the blank to complete this quote by Mahatma Gandhi.

3. When listing the countries of Africa alphabetically in English, the name of which country comes last?

4. Who succeeded the only woman president of India?

5. Which heavenly body is known as 'Lune' in French and 'Mond' in German?

6. Who is older: Anoushka Shankar or Norah Jones?

SET 9

1. A human heart can be transplanted: serious or joking?

2. Which animal's scientific name is *Varanus komodoensis*?

3. Which famous character, created by Charles Dickens, was Dora Spenlow was the first wife of?

4. Traditionally, which animals pull the sledge of Santa Claus?

5. On whose golden jubilee in 1887 was the Chhatrapati Shivaji Terminus in Mumbai formally opened?

6. Which musician was born as Robindro Shaunkor Chowdhury in Varanasi on 7 April, 1920?

SET 10

1. Hamid Ansari is the current chairman of the Rajya Sabha: serious or joking?

2. If Hero is Phantom's pet horse, what kind of an animal is Devil?

3. Whose birth anniversary is celebrated as the International Day of Non-Violence?

4. How is the margosa tree better known to us?

5. In which state is the Surajkund Crafts Mela held?

6. In which part of the body would you come across the conjunctiva?

SET 11

1. Jellyfish are fish: serious or joking?

2. In which Indian state is the Nagaur Fair held?

3. Who took the oath as president of India on 26 January, 1950?

4. Who is the first Indian player to have played in more than one hundred international football matches?

5. Who is the narrator of the novel *Gulliver's Travels*?

6. Which actress made her Hindi film debut with the 2010 film *Dabangg*?

SET 12

1. 'Jana Gana Mana' was officially adopted as India's National Anthem in 1947: serious or joking?

2. Who came into the Seeonee Wolf Pack for a bull's price and on Baloo's good word?

3. Which flower gets its name from the Swedish botanist, Andreas Dahl?

4. In the 1975 film *Sholay*, which actor asked 'Kitney aadmi thhey'?

5. The *Arabica* species of what accounts for eighty percent of its production?

6. Which state was formerly called Rajputana?

SET 13

1. Rabies is transmitted to humans from animals: serious or joking?

2. According to Hindu mythology, who is also known as Neelkanth?

3. In Olympic Games, which bird's feathers make up the sixteen feathers in a shuttlecock used to play badminton?

4. Which superhero's real name is Steve Rogers?

5. Whose tomb, exacavated by Howard Carter, revealed around 5,398 objects?

6. Which union territory of India's name in English ends with a fruit with a seed?

SET 14

1. In *The Jungle Book*, Riki Tiki Tavi is a snake: serious or joking?

2. Which colour signifies water in the emblem of the United Nations?

3. Who was the first Indian sportsperson to be featured in the famous Madame Tussauds museum?

4. In *The Dark Knight Rises*, which superhero was played by Christian Bale?

5. Which is the Inuit word for 'house'?

6. If you were writing alphabetically in English, which state would come between Punjab and Sikkim?

SET 15

1. Only male walruses have tusks: serious of joking?

2. Who served as the prime minister of India between 1984-1989?

3. Who has scored the most number of runs in the IPL till 2013?

4. Which branch of the armed services has as its motto 'Shano Varuna'?

5. Under whose directorship did the Physics department at the IISc, Bangalore came into being in 1933?

6. Who is the famous son of Rishi Kapoor and Neetu Kapoor?

SET 16

1. National Sports Day is celebrated in India on the birth anniversary of Dhyan Chand: serious or joking?

2. Your father's only sister's mother's only son is your...

3. Which Indian leader lends his name to a UNESCO World Heritage terminus at Mumbai?

4. Complete the name of this film: '_____ *and the Curse of Damyaan*'.

5. In which century was the Nobel Peace Prize first awarded?

6. The musky rat-kangaroo lives only in this continent.

SET 17

1. The colour white is common to the flags of Bangladesh and India: serious or joking?

2. In the Ramayana, who was Luv's brother?

3. What does the 'I' in 'FBI' stand for?

4. Which Indian hockey player's autobiography is *Goal*?

5. Brihadratha, who was assassinated in 185 BC, was which dynasty's last king?

6. Which American inventor founded a school in Boston to train teachers of the deaf, in 1872?

SET 18

1. Giraffes have thirty-two teeth, just like you and me: serious or joking?

2. On which colour band does the chakra appears in the National Flag of India?

3. On whose work is the train Godan Express named?

4. What is produced by the worm *Bombyx mori*?

5. In which country is the Jigme Singye Wangchuck National Park?

6. Which team holds the record of the highest innings total in a fifty over ODI match?

SET 19

1. Samurais are an ancient warrior caste of China: serious or joking?

2. What was named by Joseph Priestley when he found that it rubbed out pencil marks?

3. Which is the only state of India that starts with 'M' and ends with 'M'?

4. Who is the only British prime minister to receive a Nobel Prize for Literature?

5. Who said about whom: 'I only hope that we never lose sight of one thing—that it was all started by a mouse'?

6. Which cricketer took oath as a Rajya Sabha member in 2012?

SET 20

1 Orangutans spend most of their time in trees: serious or joking?

2. In the Ramayana, who was the mother of Lakshmana and Shatrughna?

3. The first woman cosmonaut to receive the title of 'Hero of the Soviet Union' was...

4. If it wasn't the weather or the government, what changed in Orissa on 1 November, 2011?

5. In a book, will the even numbered pages be on your right or left?

6. Which fort complex was built as the palace fort of Shahjahanabad, the new capital built by Shah Jahan?

SET 21

1. The Bharat Ratna medal is shaped like the leaf of the neem tree: serious or joking?

2. Which woman scientist wrote *Treatise on Radioactivity*?

3. Which Mughal emperor was named Salim after Sheikh Salim Chishti?

4. Name the chief minister-son of Mulayam Singh Yadav.

5. If Rajasthan is the largest state in India in terms of area, which is the second largest?

6. Which is the national aquatic animal of India?

SET 22

1. Mumbai is served by the Indira Gandhi International Airport: serious or joking?

2. Which former athlete is sometimes referred to as Payyoli Express?

3. Which letter immediately follows 'O' on a Qwerty keyboard?

4. Which director's last film was *Jab Tak Hai Jaan*?

5. How many sides does a hexagon have?

6. Who translated the national anthem of India, 'Jana Gana Mana' from Bengali to English?

SET 23

1. A scorpion has six legs: serious or joking?

2. Which fuel's miners are most commonly found with the black lung disease?

3. In the Ramayana, who was married to Urmila?

4. How many bails are used in a cricket match?

5. On the banks of which lake is Nishat Garden in Jammu and Kashmir located?

6. Which country's first president was Kemal Ataturk?

SET 24

1. 'March of the volunteers' is the national anthem of China: serious or joking?

2. Whose autobiography is titled *The Diary of a Young Girl*?

3. Which Indian union territory's name is the French interpretation of the original name meaning 'new settlement'?

4. Which is more dense: water at four degrees Celsius or ice at zero degree Celsius?

5. In the world of computers, what is generally regarded as the largest wide-area network?

6. Which tennis championship is an annual event at the Roland Garros?

SET 25

1. Pure gold is twenty-four carat gold: serious or joking?

2. In computers, what does 'Ctrl' stand for?

3. Which breed of dog is also known as German Shepherd?

4. In a rainbow, if violet is at one end, which colour is at the other?

5. 'Industry, Impartiality and Integrity' is which organisation's motto?

6. Which tennis star's autobiography is titled *Open*?

SET 26

1. A millennium refers to a peiod of hundred years: serious or joking?

2. Which Hindi film actor is popularly called Dabangg Khan?

3. In the Mahabharata, who was the eldest of the Pandavas?

4. Which was the first creature to go into space?

5. According to the Guinness World Records, which desert has the highest sand dunes in the world?

6. If BCCI is for cricket in India, then what is AIFF for?

SET 27

1. The northern white rhinoceros is white in colour: serious or joking?

2. In literature, Robinson Crusoe's companion shared his name with which day of the week?

3. The Ramon Magsaysay award is named after the president of this country.

4. On a standard computer keyboard, which number appears on the same key as the dollar sign?

5. By which name is the artificial limb provided by Bhagwan Mahaveer Viklang Sahayata Samiti known?

6. In the Mahabharata, who was the most famous son of Hiranyadhanush, the king of the foresters?

SET 28

1. Tamil Nadu is sometimes referred to as 'God's Own Country': serious or joking?

2. In the abbreviation 'UFO', what does the letter 'U' stand for?

3. Which actor, who passed away in 2012, was lovingly called Kaka?

4. In literature, what is the name of the little girl known for her adventures in 'Wonderland'?

5. Who immediately preceded the only woman president of India?

6. Which word describes the centre of the target in archery and darts?

SET 29

1. One can estimate a lion's age by the colour of it's nose: serious or joking?

2. What is the shape of the special feature on an Indian thousand rupee note, generally meant to aid the visually impaired?

3. Which city in Tamil Nadu was so named because Lord Shiva was so pleased at its sight that divine nectar fell like a blessing from his locks?

4. In 1924, which leader was appointed chief executive officer of the Calcutta Municipal Corporation?

5. Who was the first of the twelve men to walk on the surface of Earth's Moon?

6. Which film series have the characters Woody and Buzz Lightyear?

SET 30

1. Shakespeare is also known as the Bard of Avon: serious or joking?

2. What kind of a creature is Master Shifu in the film *Kung Fu Panda*?

3. The Mahesa-murti cave is the most important cave of this landmark.

4. In the Ramayana, who unintentionally killed Shravan Kumar while hunting?

5. What, of national importance, was designed by D. Udaya Kumar?

6. Agartala is the capital of which Indian state?

ANSWERS

HISTORY

1. Darjeeling
2. Grand Trunk Road
3. Tiger
4. Mahatma Gandhi
5. Rajasthan
6. Alexander the Great
7. Peshwa
8. Pakistan
9. Subhas Chandra Bose
10. Jawaharlal Nehru
11. Hyderabad
12. October
13. Shah Jahan
14. Chetak
15. Ashoka (*A-shoka* means without sorrow.)
16. Vasco da Gama

17. India Gate

18. Shivaji

19. Statue of Liberty

20. France

21. Winston Churchill

22. Jantar Mantar

23. Akbar

24. Mahavira

25. Swami Vivekananda

SCIENCE

1. Edward Jenner

2. Gold

3. Quinine

4. Eye

5. S. Chandrasekhar

6. Heart

7. Chemistry

8. Albert Einstein

9. Liver diseases

10. Neptune

11. LCD

12. Parachute

13. Tooth decay

14. Stethoscope

15. Iodine

16. Isaac Newton

17. Ctrl + S

18. Ear

19. Leonardo da Vinci

20. The @ sign

21. Kidney

22. World Wide Web

23. Microwave oven

24. Ayurveda

25. C.V. Raman

GEOGRAPHY

1. Mountain passes

2. The sunrise seen from Mount Fuji

3. Assam

4. Kilimanjaro

5. Allahabad

6. Mauritius

7. Yash Chopra

8. Bibi Ka Maqbara

9. Baghdad

10. China

11. Chhattisgarh

12. Mount Fuji

13. Narmada

14. Mount Everest

15. Odisha (It is in Bhubaneswar.)

16. Antarctica

17. Aurora Borealis

18. Brahmaputra

19. Pakistan

20. Robinson Crusoe Island

21. La Paz

22. Sutlej

23. Visakhapatnam

24. Malaysia

25. Jharkhand

LANGUAGE AND LITERATURE

1. Colon

2. *1984*

3. Gulliver

4. Plus

5. Mahatma Gandhi

6. Shylock

7. Rani Laxmi Bai

8. Tenzing Norgay

9. Aluminium

10. They all played the role of Lord Voldemort

11. Alice's sister

12. Dictionary

13. A pound of his flesh

14. Alice

15. A prison

16. Satyajit Ray

17. William Shakespeare

18. *A Tale of Two Cities* by Charles Dickens.

19. Portuguese

20. *3 Idiots*

21. *Treasure Island*

22. Botanix

23. Spider-Man

24. Panchatantra

25. Hamlet

POLITICS

1. Pranab Mukherjee

2. Voting age

3. Bangladesh

4. Ministry of External Affairs

5. Parliament House

6. S. Radhakrishnan

7. C. Rajagopalachari

8. Indira Gandhi (For a year from 1969 to 1970.)

9. Barack Obama
10. Jawaharlal Nehru
11. Afghanistan
12. Jawaharlal Nehru (Vijaya Lakshmi Pandit)
13. Bangladesh
14. S. Radhakrishnan
15. Barack Obama
16. Russia
17. Morarji Desai
18. Shanti Van
19. Adolf Hitler
20. Vijaya Lakshmi Pandit
21. Aung San Suu Kyi
22. Rajiv Gandhi
23. World War I
24. Bhutan
25. Nelson Mandela

ENTERTAINMENT

1. Rajinikanth
2. *Bunty Aur Babli*
3. Duffli
4. Hrithik Roshan
5. Phantom
6. Salman Khan

7. *Ek Tha Tiger*
8. Dog
9. Ravi Shankar
10. Mickey Mouse
11. Abhishek Bachchan
12. Riteish Deshmukh
13. Garfield
14. *Dilwale Dulhania Le Jayenge* (Salman Khan suggested the name for *Taare Zameen Par.*)
15. Farhan Akhtar
16. Bhimsen Joshi
17. Hobbes
18. Rahul Bose
19. Amitabh Bachchan
20. Kamal Haasan
21. Manna Dey
22. Sridevi
23. Sonam Kapoor
24. Chacha Chaudhary
25. *Maine Pyar Kyun Kiya*

SPORTS

1. Virender Sehwag
2. Cricket
3. Saina Nehwal

4. Score a goal

5. Cannot be ruled offside

6. Manchester United

7. Zimbabwe

8. Ranjitsinhji

9. Ricky Ponting

10. Twice

11. Hyderabad

12. India

13. Mark Boucher

14. India

15. Lionel Messi

16. New Zealand

17. Judo

18. M.S. Dhoni

19. Marathon (26.2 miles)

20. Yuvraj Singh (Father: Yograj Singh)

21. When a batsman is out on the first ball he faces

22. Brendon McCullum

23. Yellow and red cards

24. Boxing

25. Athletics

RELIGION AND MYTHOLOGY

1. Buddha

2. Krishna

3. Ravana

4. Sikhism

5. Karna

6. Hanuman (*Hanu* means 'jawbone'.)

7. Delhi

8. Ramayana

9. Sita

10. Eyes of the gods

11. Shiva

12. Ramayana

13. Gandhari

14. Ganesha

15. Lap

16. Vishnu

17. Brahma

18. Sikhism

19. Vishwakarma

20. Kaushalya

21. Veda Vyasa

22. Musical instruments

23. Buddhism

24. Bhima

25. Rama

NATURE AND WILDLIFE

1. Giraffe

2. Indonesia

3. Dog

4. Cotton

5. Insides of the mouth

6. It is the smallest squirrel

7. Vampire bats

8. Kangaroos

9. Quinine (The Quechua name is *quina quina* meaning 'bark of barks'.)

10. Green anaconda

11. Giant panda

12. Sikkim

13. The sound made by its wings

14. Kiwi

15. Lion

16. Born Free

17. Dolphin (Derived from the word *delphis*.)

18. Eyes

19. Bats

20. Cheetah

21. Hummingbird

22. Nepal

23. Snail

24. Date palm
25. Kiwi

ART AND CULTURE

1. White
2. Rangoli
3. Zakir Hussain
4. Koodiyaattam
5. Tamil Nadu
6. Sherwani
7. Mandolin (Ghatam is a percussion instrument and shehnai and bansuri are wind instruments.)
8. Ravi Shankar
9. Diwali
10. Nawab Wajid Ali Shah
11. Ankle
12. Bharatanatyam
13. Amjad Ali Khan
14. Kerala
15. Arjuna and Draupadi
16. Japan
17. Amjad Ali Khan
18. Holi
19. Zakir Hussain
20. Gujarat

21. Classical music
22. Krishna
23. Mukhda
24. Zakir Hussain
25. Ravi Shankar

FOOD

1. China
2. Orange
3. V. Kurien
4. Gulab jamun
5. Potato
6. Root
7. Jammu and Kashmir
8. Gulab jamun
9. Bhujia
10. Basmati rice
11. Boiling
12. Ginger
13. Jalebi
14. Chillies
15. Clove
16. Jammu and Kashmir
17. Pasta
18. Kulfi

19. Goa

20. Bread crumbs

21. Sugar

22. Barfi

23. Popped popcorn

24. Guava

25. Potato

GENERAL

1. Nylon

2. Eyes

3. Ten thousand

4. Pleated salwars

5. Red

6. Mountaineering

7. Nothing

8. Surma

9. Green

10. Mother Teresa

11. Slides down chimneys

12. A stamp (The three-shilling stamp was first issued in Sweden in 1855 and used in 1857 to mail a letter.)

13. The dragon

14. Boat

15. Law

16. Akashvani

17. Red

18. Aquamarine

19. Positive influence on America's eating habits

20. Mother Teresa

21. Snake

22. United Nations

23. Gangnam Style (By Psy)

24. Aadhaar

25. Myanmar

SUPEROVER

SET 1

1. Joking. It is the Hindi name for cinnamon.

2. Meghdoot

3. Sambar

4. Great Wall of China

5. Marie Curie

6. Usain Bolt

SET 2

1. Serious

2. Oliver Twist

3. Christopher Columbus
4. Kings XI Punjab
5. Yen
6. Republic Day

SET 3

1. Serious
2. Two
3. Jawaharlal Nehru
4. Krishna
5. Viswanathan Anand
6. One thousand and fifty gm of cotton

SET 4

1. Serious
2. Lotus Temple
3. Australia
4. Santa Claus
5. *Hamlet*
6. Kolkata

SET 5

1. Serious
2. Varanasi

5. Macbeth

4. Jewellery

5. Cycle

6. Chhota Bheem

SET 6

1. Joking

2. Spider

3. Apple

4. Lakshadweep

5. Viticulture

6. Bhutan

SET 7

1. Scrious

2. Kareena Kapoor

3. Bahadur Shah Zafar

4. Pawn

5. Mount Everest

6. Hanuman

SET 8

1. Joking; green, blue and yellow also.

2. Blind

3. Zimbabwe
4. Pranab Mukherjee
5. Moon
6. Norah Jones

SET 9

1. Serious
2. Komodo dragon
3. David Copperfield
4. Reindeer
5. Queen Victoria. It was formerly known as the Victoria Terminus.
6. Ravi Shankar

SET 10

1. Serious
2. Wolf
3. Mahatma Gandhi
4. Neem tree
5. Haryana
6. Eyes

SET 11

1. Joking

2. Rajasthan
3. Rajendra Prasad
4. Baichung Bhutia
5. Gulliver himself
6. Sonakshi Sinha

SET 12

1. Joking. It was adopted in 1950.
2. Mowgli
3. Dahlia
4. Amjad Khan
5. Coffee
6. Rajasthan

SET 13

1. Serious
2. Shiva
3. Goose
4. Captain America
5. Tutankhamun
6. Puducherry

SET 14

1. Joking; mongoose.

4. White
3. Sachin Tendulkar
4. Batman/ Bruce Wayne
5. Igloo
6. Rajasthan

SET 15

1. Joking
2. Rajiv Gandhi
3. Suresh Raina
4. Indian Navy
5. C.V. Raman
6. Ranbir Kapoor

SET 16

1. Serious
2. Father
3. Shivaji
4. Chhota Bheem
5. Twentieth
6. Australia

SET 17

1. Joking; green.

2. Kusha

3. Investigation

4. Dhyan Chand

5. Maurya

6. Alexander Graham Bell

SET 18

1. Serious

2. White

3. Premchand

4. Silk

5. Bhutan

6. Sri Lanka

SET 19

1. Joking; Japan.

2. Rubber

3. Mizoram

4. Winston Churchill

5. Walt Disney about Mickey Mouse

6. Sachin Tendulkar

SET 20

1. Serious

2.   Sumitra
3.   Valentina Tereshkova
4.   The name
5.   Left
6.   Red Fort

SET 21

1.   Joking; peepul.
2.   Marie Curie
3.   Jahangir
4.   Akhilesh Yadav
5.   Madhya Pradesh
6.   Ganges river dolphin

SET 22

1.   Joking. It is in New Delhi.
2.   P.T. Usha
3.   P
4.   Yash Chopra
5.   Six
6.   Rabindranath Tagore

SET 23

1.   Joking. It has eight legs.

2. Coal

3. Lakshmana

4. Four

5. Dal Lake

6. Turkey

SET 24

1. Serious

2. Anne Frank

3. Puducherry

4. Water at four degrees Celsius

5. Internet

6. French Open

SET 25

1. Serious

2. Control

3. Alsatian

4. Red

5. CBI (Central Bureau of Investigation)

6. Andre Agassi

SET 26

1. Joking; thousand.

2. Salman Khan
3. Yudhishthira
4. A dog. The name of the dog was Laika.
5. Sahara. In Isaouane-n-Tifernine in east-central Algeria, the dunes can reach a height of 465 m (1,526 ft).
6. Football

SET 27

1. Joking. Its actually more of a battleship grey or, sometimes, a latte-brown.
2. Friday
3. The Philippines
4. 4
5. Jaipur Foot
6. Ekalavya

SET 28

1. Joking
2. Unidentified
3. Rajesh Khanna
4. Alice
5. A.P.J. Abdul Kalam
6. Bullseye

SET 29

1. Serious
2. Diamond
3. Madurai
4. Subhas Chandra Bose
5. Neil Armstrong
6. *Toy Story*

SET 30

1. Serious
2. Red panda
3. Elephanta Caves
4. Dasharatha
5. Rupee sign
6. Tripura